This Little Tiger
book belongs to:

_____

_____

To Julia and
Paul, fellow billy
goats . . . and to Mom, for
playing the best troll who lived
under the bridge at Umstead Park ~ M A

For Caleb *x*
~ K P

LITTLE TIGER PRESS LTD
an imprint of the Little Tiger Group
1 The Coda Centre, 189 Munster Road,
London SW6 6AW
www.littletiger.co.uk

First published in Great Britain 2014

Text by Mara Alperin
Text copyright © Little Tiger Press 2014
Illustrations copyright © Kate Pankhurst 2014
Kate Pankhurst has asserted her right to be
identified as the illustrator of this work under the
Copyright, Designs and Patents Act, 1988
A CIP catalogue record for this book is
available from the British Library

ISBN 978-1-84895-685-8
Printed in China
LTP/1900/1773/1216
10 9 8 7 6 5 4

The Three Billy Goats Gruff

Mara Alperin

Illustrated by Kate Pankhurst

LITTLE TIGER PRESS
London

High in the mountains lived three billy goats.
They were called Baby Gruff, Middle Gruff
and Big Gruff.

All winter long an icy wind blew, and the billy goats ate only dry thistles and scraggly brambles. When at last the snow melted, they set off for the valley below.

Down the mountain they trotted, **trip! trap! trip! trap!**
to the old stone bridge. There, on the other side
of the river, was the freshest, greenest
grass they had ever seen.

Look at that yummy-scrummy grass!

And so the billy goats lined up to cross the bridge – first Baby Gruff, then Middle Gruff, then Big Gruff.

But under the bridge, hiding in the shadows, was a BIG, ugly troll!

He had a **terrible** warty face.

He had **horrible** pointy ears.

RIVER RECIPES FOR TROLLS

He had awful, **stinky** breath.

And he liked to eat **anyone** who crossed his bridge!

So when Baby Gruff skipped across the bridge with a **trip! trap! trip!** . . .

the troll sprang up from below, snarling and slobbering.

"It's me," Baby Gruff squealed. "The littlest billy goat! I'm going to the meadow to nibble all the flowers."

"Oh no, you're not!" roared the troll. "This is MY bridge. And I'm going to eat you up for breakfast, with some freshly buttered toast!"

Baby Gruff trembled. "Please don't eat me!" he squeaked. "I'm so little, you wouldn't even taste me! Wait for my older brother, Middle Gruff. He's bigger and *much* tastier."

The troll licked his lips. "Bigger? Tastier?" he cried. "Then I'll eat him instead. Now BE GONE WITH YOU!"

And so Baby Gruff
scurried over the bridge.

 Trip!

Trap!

Trip!

"Silly old troll," he giggled.

Soon after, Middle Gruff clattered across the old stone bridge, **trippity-trap! trippity-trap!**

The troll leaped up once more, growling . . .

Who's that trip-trapping

over **my** bridge?

"It's me," Middle Gruff bleated. "The next billy goat! I'm going to the meadow to munch all the grass."

"**Oh no, you're not!**" roared the troll. "I'm going to gobble you up for breakfast, with a nice glass of milk!"

"Don't be silly," cried Middle Gruff. "I'm so boney, I'd make your teeth fall out. Wait for my older brother, Big Gruff. He's fatter and *much* yummier."

The troll started to drool. "Fatter? Yummier?" he shouted. "Then I'll eat him instead."

Now **BE GONE WITH YOU!**

And so Middle Gruff trotted
across the bridge.

Trippity-trap!

Trippity-trap!

"Silly old troll!" he tutted.

Finally, Big Gruff thundered up to the bridge.

TRIP! TRAP! TROMP!

"**RAARGH!**" roared the troll.
"Who's that trip-trapping over **my** bridge?"

He was very, VERY hungry by now!

Big Gruff stomped his hooves.
    "It's me," he grunted. "The biggest billy goat."

The troll's tummy was rumbling and grumbling. Up he jumped, bellowing . . .

Here I come to GOBBLE YOU UP!

"NO!" said Big Gruff, pointing his big, strong horns right at the troll.

"HERE I COME!"

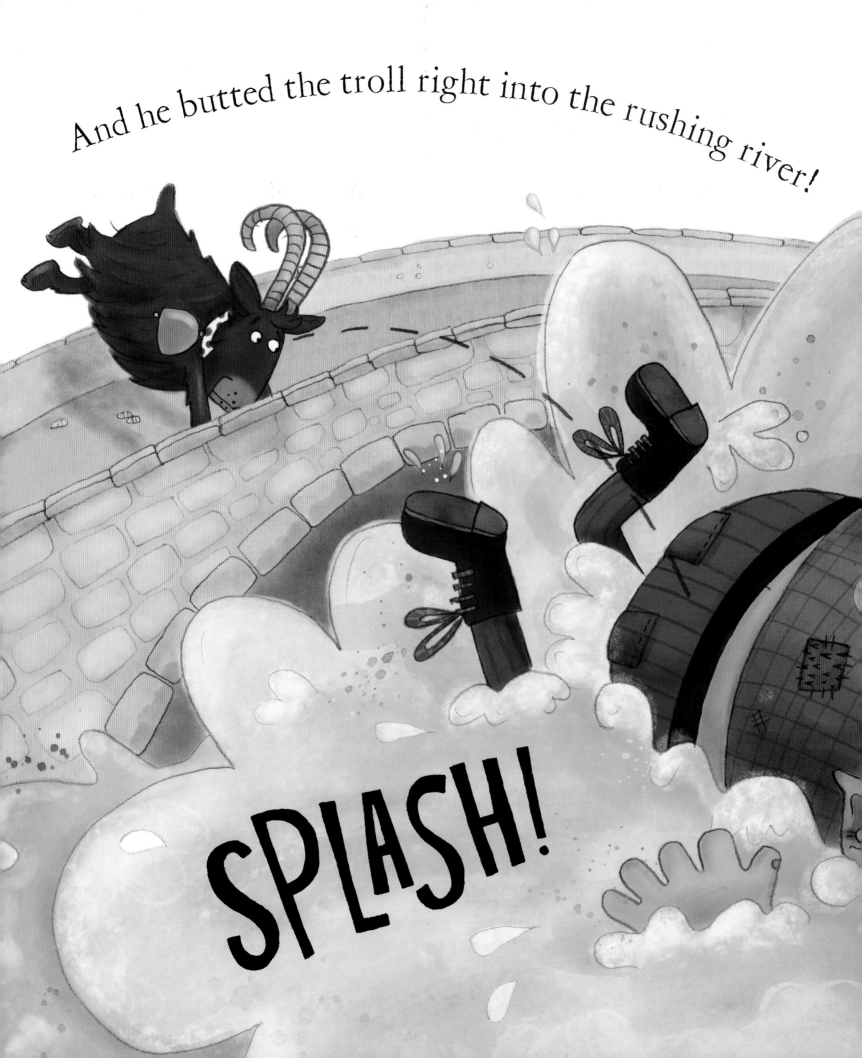

"AARRGHH!"

howled the troll as the river swept him far away.

And so Big Gruff thudded over the bridge to join his brothers in the meadow.

TRIP!

TRAP!

TROMP!

"Silly old troll," he chuckled.

All summer long, the three billy goats Gruff crunched and munched the delicious green grass, until they could eat no more. And they never, ever saw that **silly** old troll again!

My First Fairy Tales

are familiar, fun and friendly stories – with a marvellously modern twist!